SCOOBY-DOO!

AND THE

Haunted Diner

By Mariah Balaban
Illustrated by Duendes del Sur

WORLDWIDE PUBLISHING

SCHOLASTIC INC.
New York Toronto London Auckland
Sydney Mexico City New Delhi Hong Kong

ISBN: 978-0-545-20882-6

Designed by Michael Massen

12 11 10 9 8 7 6 5 4 3 2 1   10 11 12 13 14 15/0

Printed in U.S.A.
First printing, January 2010   40

The Mystery Machine bounced down the highway.

Scooby-Doo and the gang were taking a road trip.

Velma pointed at the sky. "Look at those dark clouds. I think a storm is coming."

They heard a loud rumble.

"Jinkies!" exclaimed Velma. "That thunder sure is loud!"

"Like, that's not thunder, that's my tummy rumbling!" Shaggy moaned. "I'm starving!"

"Re, roo!" Scooby barked.

Fred noticed a sign for a diner. He pulled the Mystery Machine into the parking lot.

The gang sat down and looked at the menu.
Scooby and Shaggy were excited.
"We'll have veggie burgers, French fries,
pizza, and onion rings," Shaggy said.
"Ron't rorget the rilkshakes!" Scooby added.

Outside the diner, it was as dark as night.
"Jeepers! This storm is terrible," said
Daphne. "It's a good thing we pulled over."
BOOM! Thunder shook the diner.
CRACK! Lightning lit up the sky.

Suddenly, the lights went out.
"Ruh-roh!" said Scooby.
"The storm must have knocked down a power line," said Velma.

"The lights will be back on soon," Shaggy told Scooby. "There's nothing to worry about, buddy."

A spooky moan filled the air.
AAAAAAA-WHOOOOOO!
It sounded like a monster!
"Like, on second thought, start worrying!"
cried Shaggy.

Scooby and Shaggy raced to the kitchen to hide from the monster.

"No sense hiding on an empty stomach," Shaggy whispered. "Let's find some grub."

"Ruh-huh!" Scooby agreed.

"It sure is spooky in here, Scoob," Shaggy said.

He felt around in the dark and found a drawer. There was a flashlight inside.

"Now we can see our way to the refrigerator," Shaggy said.
"Raggy, rook," gulped Scooby-Doo.
The refrigerator wasn't all they saw. . . .

It was a ghost!
"Like, time to make like a banana and split!" cried Shaggy.

The lights came back on.
Scooby and Shaggy looked around.
"The ghost is gone," Shaggy said.

But so was the gang!
"Oh, no! The ghost must have gotten them," Shaggy cried. "Let's get out of here before it gets us, too!"

"Run ror rit, Raggy!" Scooby yelped.
Scooby and Shaggy dashed out of
the diner as quickly as they could.

"Let's hide in here," Shaggy suggested.
The cellar was dark and damp. It
looked too spooky for Scooby.
    "That ghost will never find us now!"
said Shaggy.

Scooby and Shaggy heard a ghostly howl. It was calling their names!

"SCOOOOOOBY! SHAAAAAAAGGY!"

Shaggy and Scooby's teeth chattered. Their knees knocked together.

The cellar doors opened slowly.
CREEEEAAAAAK!

"It was nice knowing you, Scoob!" Shaggy whispered.

A spooky shadow fell over them. Shaggy and Scooby looked up.

"Rikes! Rit's a ritch!" barked Scooby-Doo. The witch stood at the top of the stairs. She pointed a long, bony finger at them. "Like, we're goners now!" gulped Shaggy.

At that moment, Fred, Daphne, and
Velma appeared.

"Daphne, Fred, Velma!" Shaggy waved
to them. "Help us! But, like, look out for
the witch!"

"It's not a witch, silly," Daphne said. "It's the waitress from the diner!"
The woman pulled back her hood and smiled. "This is my rain poncho."

"What on earth are you two doing?" asked Velma. "We've been looking everywhere for you!"

"We were hiding," Shaggy told her. "This diner is haunted!"

"Haunted?" said Fred.

"First we heard a monster moaning in the diner when the lights went out," Shaggy said. "That was just the jukebox powering down," explained the waitress. "The record sounds funny when it slows down like that."

"Well then, what about the ghost in the kitchen?" asked Shaggy. "It chased us out and then kidnapped you guys!"

"I can explain that," said the cook. "I was
in the kitchen when the lights went out. In
the dark, I knocked a bag of flour all over
myself. I must have looked pretty scary!"

"And we weren't kidnapped!" Velma added. "We just went out to the van to get flashlights."

"What about the ghost calling our names in the cellar?" Shaggy asked.

"That was us looking for you," Fred explained. "The wind made our voices sound spooky."

"So the diner isn't haunted after all," Shaggy sighed. "What a relief! But there is still one more mystery left to solve."

"What's that?" Fred asked.

"Like, when do we eat? We're starving!" Shaggy joked.

The cook got to work. Soon the waitress came out of the kitchen holding a huge tray piled high with food.

"Five veggie burger and French fry combos and two extra-large milkshakes!"

"Scooby-Dooby-Doo!" barked Scooby-Doo.

Make Your Own Scooby Snacks!
Remember to ask an adult for help!

Ingredients

2 cups plain flour
1 cup oatmeal
1/2 cup sugar
1/4 pound butter
1/2 cup cocoa
2 eggs
2 tablespoons vanilla extract
2 tablespoons walnut extract

Directions

1. Preheat the oven to 350 degrees.
2. Add all ingredients into a large bowl and mix with a wooden spoon. You may need to add a little milk if the mixture is a little dry.
3. Grease a large baking tray. Using a tablespoon, take a spoonful of the mixture and flatten onto the baking tray. Use a cookie cutter to make the shape you want.
4. Bake in the oven for 8 minutes. If the snacks need more time, put them back in the oven for another few minutes.*
5. Using a spatula, place snacks on a wire rack to cool.

* How do you like your Scooby Snacks? Bake them for a little less for chewier snacks, and a little longer for crisp snacks.